THE GIRL WHO NEVER CAME BACK

ANGEL BANSAL

People who motivated me in my journey

Firstly, I would like the thank my really hardworking Principal ma'am Ms. Ashu Tyagi who motivated me and supported me. Thankyou Ma'am for always helping us. You are the best example of a perfect principal.

My elder sister, my role-model Vaishnavi Bansal. Thank you for always inspiring me and also supporting me in my journey.

Love you sister!

My friend Ishi Aggarwal (The Magical Rhymes) who always used to help me to find faults in my content and make my book better. She is an amazing poet. Thankyou little sista for always supporting me.

I would also like to thank Aarchi Advani di for helping me a lot in getting my 1st book published....Thank you so much! Means a lot to me.

Contents

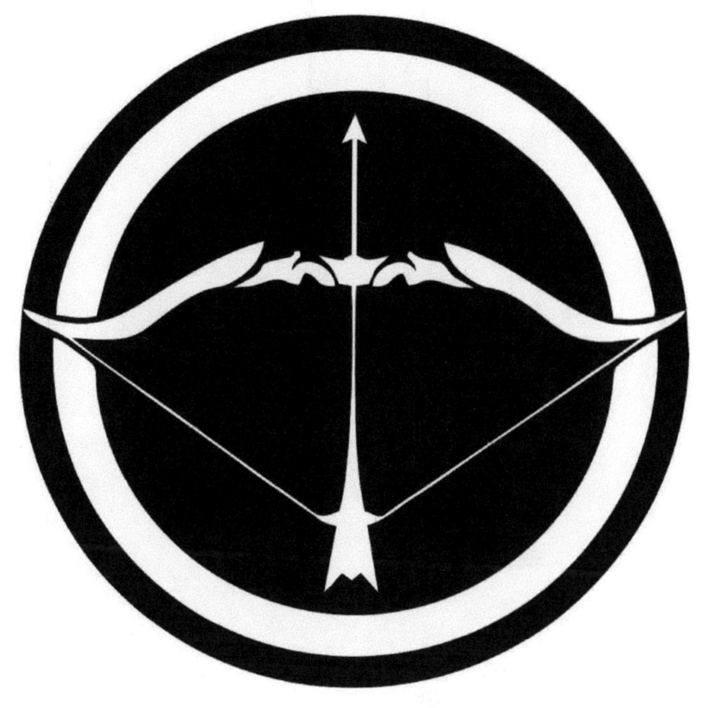

A book by

Penaaki

ONE

Once I had a thought that what would happen if aliens exist for real? It was just a thought but soon after some days it was discovered that something strange was coming towards earth. Soon the spread all over the world. The research departments were busy finding word about it all the news channels were suffused by the news of space-ships and aliens. Some were saying that it's the end of the human era. Suddenly one day something strange (a kind of spaceship) appeared in the sky. Everyone was so intimidated that people locked themselves in the house. The scientists and the researchers were in a great chaos because they have not seen any such thing before. It was dark in the sky due to the big spaceship blocking the sunlight. The wind was blowing and the trees were shaking due to the blowing wind and the spaceship was coming closer and closer as if it is going to land and it crash- landed in a jungle. The people were so scared and after some time it was publicized that the alien who came in the spaceship has been caught by the government and now people can relax because there is nothing to worry about.

But now the question was that if the alien is really caught so what should be done with him? So the government advertised that the research department is in need of some person who is ready to risk his life as they were in need of someone who could talk to the alien and for that a liquid drug has to be injected in his body due to which some changes might occur in the person's body and there were chances that he may lose his life but the government will be giving a huge amount of money to the person who would do this. The rumour spread like fire. Everyone in the country was talking about it. But the reality was something else, the alien girl was still out there. She was roaming in the jungle. Her name was (Gillis Cal Quiso Cara Cara Number Twenty) I know it's a bit strange but yes that was her name. She came on earth with a mission that was to observe the people of earth and collect information about them. She was a girl with super-powers.

TWO

She looked the same as humans only her dressing sense was a bit different as compared to that of human beings. She entered the city and dressed herself like other people. She looked the exact same as humans by appearance that no-one could judge her and find out that she was an alien and not a human being.

On the other hand, a girl belonging to a middle-class family found out about the prize money. She was a youngster and was badly in need of money. Her mom has divorced her dad 10 years back as he was a womanizer, he used to harass her mum and he married another woman, so her mom and she have left him. It needs a lot of courage for a woman who have never faced the world to take such a big step.

But this shows that her mom was a bold woman after that her mom took a small room on rent by selling her two gold bangles which her mom's mother gave her in her marriage. She also took a sewing machine on rent and started to stitch clothes. She was very good at that as when she was small her mom taught her how to stitch. She used to stitch everything weather it was a cloth bag or skirt, a gown or a blouse, a shirt or a pant every single thing. At the beginning they faced many challenges and many hurdles but she didn't lose hope and worked hard day and night.

The young little girl who was only 9 years old didn't went to school from the time they left her dad as they were not having enough money to fulfil the basic requirements so her mom could not afford this luxury. She used to manage all the household work alone as her mom used to work hard to stitch clothes day and night. After one and half year of great struggle they finally bought a small home. And the girl was sent to a school.

Her mom was the only earner left in the house she used to manage everything alone. The little girl after returning from school tried her best to find a way and help her mom. One by one years passed, and they started to live a normal life. Ten years flew like very fast, and they started to live a normal life. The little girl has now grown into a beautiful 19year old woman. Everything was going good but suddenly one day the young girl's mom fell ill and collapsed. The young girl was so scared and called the ambulance. The ambulance arrived in few minutes and after some time they were there in the hospital. The nurses took her in a room and some tests were done and after few hours the reports arrived, and it was found that her mum was suffering from a severe lung cancer a needed an immediate surgery.

When the doctor told the girl about her mom's disease she was completely broken. It was like her entire world was scattered and her heart was broken into pieces. She was so much disturbed after hearing this, but she could not lose her hope as her mother was her everything, the only precious thing she had in her life. But you know, the sad part was they were not having enough money for the surgery of her mum. But she still she didn't lose hope and decided to go out and hunt for a job. The girl told her mom that she will arrange money from somewhere, so not to worry but the girl herself didn't know that how this would happen. She applied for some job interviews, but nothing helped her. But one day when she was sitting so some people were talking something about aliens and one of them said that the prize money is 70 lakh and this suddenly caught her attention from her lost and broken world, she suddenly stood and ran toward those people and asked them about the prize money. So, she decided to apply for the mission. She must reach the government for this mission, it was bit risky, but she decided to it for her mother.

She was a little happy, but she didn't know that reaching the government was not that easy process. The first day she went to the place where people were being interviewed for the same. There she saw a long queue of people standing but she could spot not a single woman other than her. She stood in the queue for her turn the whole day, firstly in the bright sun and then finally after standing for 5 hours he stepped inside the place and then secondly for another 5 hours she waited inside but unfortunately, she was disappointed and went back home. Next day, with a new hope she went to that place again.

THREE

Today it was her lucky strike and without waiting for so long she got a chance to meet the interviewer. She took a deep breath "huffffffffffffffffhhhhh" and then went inside the room with a confident smile and positive attitude. Although she was a bit nervous inside, but she didn't let her nervousness show up on her face. The young girl was very innocent, kind and above all she was very pretty. She was having beautiful brown curly hair and a joyful smile. When she met the interviewer, he suddenly asked a question without even looking at her and giving her a chance to introduce her. The interviewer asked "Why do you agree to do this mission even when you know that you can even lose your life in the mission? But the girl without getting hesitated confidently replied and told the interviewer about her sick mom and the money she wanted for her surgery. While the girl was replying the interviewer heard that it is a voice of a girl so he slowly lifted his face up open his eyes and saw the young girl. And he could not stop himself from seeing her and kept on looking at her until she finished replying and said "Sir, are you fine? The interviewer who was greatly attracted by the young girl's beauty now thought of misusing the girl for his own benefit.

He pretended in front of her as if he is offering her the job of mission that she applied for. The man (interviewer) finalized the agreement with the girl and asked her to work for them for the amount of money she required, and he stood up and hugged the girl. The girl although didn't like that hug much but she just ignored it because she was happy for her mum. The girl who was very much in need of money agreed to the agreement at once.

The alien girl in whose name the government lied, and that small lie of government was going to get a big trouble to the young girl was still out there and the alien girl has not learnt the language which is spoken by the people on earth very fast with the help of her superpowers. She also got herself an apartment and started to work as a Dietitian in the hospital named 'Spring Edge Care. She learned everything very fast and got herself an identity and that too with her superpowers. She gave herself, a new name i.e., Monica Wilson. It was her first day in the hospital and everyone was so surprised to see her working because she worked so fast and could to the work of 10 to 15 people all alone. She managed to take care and look after more than twenty patients alone and still was never tired. It was although not a big deal for her as she could use her superpowers but for others it was like a big shock. On the very first day she made a good image of hers in the hospital. There lived a patient in a hospital named Uncle John. He was bossy in nature so one day when Monica saw him shouting on someone, so she asked a nurse who is this? And why is he shouting? So, the nurse told her about Uncle John that he was in the hospital now for more than 10 years, the hospital was now a kind of home to him now as all knew him very well the staff as well as the members of the hospital. It was not like he didn't have children, but Uncle John was suffering from a disease.

10 years back his son brought him to the hospital for a check-up but when he found out that his dad was suffering from that disease, so he left him there. He came to meet him once or twice but after he found out that his dad's condition was getting critical, so he left him there and never came to meet him or take him back. Monica felt bad for Uncle John now so she went to him and sat in his room and introduced herself to him and told her that she is new in the hospital. On the very first day he didn't talk much to her.

The young girl who was happy returned home and told her mom about the job. Her mom loved her very much so she first refused her as she was concerned about her daughter and asked her not to do it as it was dangerous, but the girl somehow manage to convince her and promised her that nothing will happen to her and she will safely return back home. She asked her mom to trust her.

The alien girl has learned and known many things about the earth and people of earth.

Two- three days passed, and Monica has somehow managed to be friendly with uncle John. She now daily used to prepare some healthy juice for uncle and used to give it to him. Now they both have started to talk to each other. So, one day Monica asked uncle about what happened before his son left him there and why did uncle never tried to contact his son or go back home again. So, uncle told him that the last words his son told him when his last came to meet him were 'SORRY DAD'. Uncle said that he wonders that if he really wanted to leave him there so why was he feeling sorry that day, but he had not get the answer to this question till now.

FOUR

On that same evening the alien girl (Monica) went out to buy some food stuff from the nearby market, on the way back to home she saw a man trashing his employ badly with a stick because of a small mistake that he made. The girl tried to stop him, but he pushed her and she got her head hit by the pole. She secretively used her superpowers and the man fell in a drain nearby. Now she understood that all the people on earth are not as good as they pretend to be, but they are cruel and barbarous.

She went home and locked herself in the room and with the help of her powers she went to the place from where she could contact to her planet. She told the head general of her planet about the cruel and selfish behaviour and acts of earthlings. Also, he asked her not to use her superpowers again in front of earthlings i.e. people of earth. If she broke this rule again then she would get a severe punishment.

The next day, the interviewer came to the young girl's house and asked her to sign some papers son that they can work forward and process as fast as possible and the innocent girl signed the papers without even reading them. The man before leaving the place told the girl that once the process is done so she would be informed and called the young girl simply replied "ok" no problem I will surely give my best, and the man left the place.

In the hospital, Monica has a new patient today, but he was not an ordinary one he was a very famous sportsperson named Alex, who got injured while playing some days back. He has already been treated but he has not recovered completely but he has become so week, but he didn't eat well so now he has been brought under Monica's surveillance. Her work was not only to plan a proper diet for him but also monitoring that is he eating well or not. So, Alex was now given the food only which Monica instructed. He was a sportsperson but still he was different from others, he loved to paint as well as read stories. So, as he was in the hospital for so long now, so he used to paint in his free time during the day and while he used to paint he was so lost in his own world and wanted no one to disturb him. so, when Monica came to see that weather he ate his food or not so she found out that the food was kept on the side table and he was lost making his painting. So, she came inside the room sat there and asked him to eat first and then he can make his painting, but he refused that he didn't want to eat. So, she stood up and came to see that what was he drawing? She saw that he has painted a very beautiful scene of space. So, she remembers of her planet cape-town on her first look to his painting.

She asked him where to have you learned it from. So, Alex replies "I have not learned it from somewhere, but I paint whatever I think or imagine. So, Monica says the stars at night look the same from planet cape- town. Aa.......ae she suddenly shuts off. But Alex suddenly spotted cape-town? What is that place? So, Monica suddenly changes the topic and says we will talk about it later now when your drawing is complete eat your food now. Alex finishes his food now.

The young girl has now started to stitch some clothes which she learnt from her mom. She used to stitch some cloth bags and sometimes even dresses for women so that meanwhile she is being called by the interviewer she could earn some money and make her mom eat some good food which is good for her health.

Monica went home and reported the head general that people on earth are really good at drawing and some of them are even childish but kind. The head general told her, good job! Gillis Quiso Cara Cara Number Twenty, collect more information and keep reporting.

FIVE

The young girl was now working so hard, she was only praying to God that everything goes well and she could somehow save her mom. Whereas on the other hand her mom was happy to see her daughter caring about her so much. Sometimes when her mom sees her daughter who was so close to her heart working so hard just to provide a good treatment to her, she got tears in her eyes she thought that her daughter who was her little princess some days back has grown so fast and become so much responsible now. Her mom was really proud of her little daughter, but she was tensed as well when she saw her girl working all the time and not even sleeping properly. She was worried that what would happen to her daughter after she dies or who will look after her daughter?

Monica and Alex have now become good friends. They used to talk and laugh together. They used to talk for hours. Alex used to tell Monica and other staff in the hospital his imaginative stories, he was really good at telling stories. Sometimes after listening to his stories Monica often thought that is, he some secret agent from planet cape-town because his stories sounded so real that is was hard to believe for her that he was an earthling and not an alien like her. Monica also used to tell stories to him about her planet.

One day Alex asked Monica that why do you always talk about cape town and Aliens only?

So, like always Monica suddenly changed the topic but Alex understood that something was strange with her because whenever he asked her about planet cape- town so she changes the topic.

So again asked her, Why do you always change the topic whenever I talk about cape-town so she replied, it is not like that may be I have been telling stories about aliens these days because of the news going all around about aliens and the spaceship that appeared few days back and Monica suddenly left the room pretending as if she got a call and got to do some urgent work.

"O My God! Hufffffffff, he almost found it about my identity but I somehow managed to save myself.

So, 2-3 days passed and now it was almost the time for Alex to leave the hospital as he has recovered. The hospital staff was helping him to pack his stuff as he has been in the hospital for a long time now.

So, he was about to leave and asked her new friend Monica to stay in touch. But Monica looked tensed because she could not tell him that she came to this planet just for a mission and could leave the planet anytime. But she gave him a gift. It was a locket that had a very precious blue colour sapphire that was of her planet.

Alex said. "Wow it is so pretty, But I cannot take it as it looks really costly. He thought so because he has never seen such stone.

But Monica replied, "No it is not like that please take it, it is a small token of love from me to you. And look I am also wearing the same.

"ha ha" Alex replied with a laughter. Okay but in return I also want to give you something.

He brought something from his bag. And guess what it was...

It was a very beautiful painting of Monica that he has made, and Monica was very much overwhelmed after looking at it and thanked Alex for the painting.

Alex also gave Monica the tickets of his game that is going to held next week and asked her to visit it. And Monica with a smile replied "Thank you! I'll surely visit, and Alex left.

SIX

The next day the young girl's mom became very sick, and the girl took her to the hospital. It was the same hospital where the alien girl (Monica Wilson) worked. She saw that the girl was badly crying. The alien girl sensed with her powers that her mom is going to die soon if see didn't get a sudden treatment so, she sneakily went in the room where she was admitted and made her well. Then she saw the girl talking on her phone about the alien and spaceship and at the same time girl was looking tensed because she didn't want to leave her mom alone. But when the young girl came to know from the doctor that now her mom condition is just fine, and she is stable so she left the hospital. She looked as if she was in a hurry Monica followed the young girl.

Monica saw the girl meeting a man (the man was actually the interviewer). The interviewer with the bad intentions was going to hug the young girl but she suddenly brought her hand forward and greeted him with a handshake. The young girl was feeling really uncomfortable and was not liking the way the interviewer used to touch her again and but she kept calm because she thought that it is not the time to think about herself, but she has to think about her mom. She felt unsecure but still she tried to stay bold. So, there they went to a café talked for a while, they ordered a coffee the man explained the girl about all her work and everything she had to do and finally they stood up and the man gave the girl an address to visit and meanwhile all this was happening Monica was watching all this hidden behind the tree from so far with the help of her powers. Now the girl took an auto rickshaw and went to that address that the man gave her. The place was very quiet and secluded, she could hardly see anyone there. The girl was a little afraid, but she collected all her courage and thought about her mum and went inside, it was a kind of old office and it looked like the place was kept closed and no one has worked there for years as the benches were all broken and dusty and the computers were not there only some waste technical equipment were all scattered everywhere all around. It was all dark inside. Suddenly someone locked the door, the girl could now see four men coming towards her, but she didn't know what to do now? But one thing was clear she understood by now That she was in great danger. She tried to escape but she could not. Monica saw all this happening with the girl, but she was so confused what to do because she couldn't use her superpowers in front of everyone. The girl hit one of the men with a wooden plank and tried to run but the other three man caught her and didn't let her escape. But after struggling for some time, she knew that this was the end. Monica could not resist herself from protecting the young girl so she came forward and tried to use her superpowers but as her general told her that if she used her superpowers again in front of earthlings her powers would be taken away and the same thing happened. Her powers were gone now but she didn't lose hope she was a strong woman, so she fought very bravely. A new hope took birth within the young girl too she thought that they could save themselves now but suddenly a man hit Monica on her head very hardly with a steel rod and she fainted. The young girl was now totally broken into tears she shouted as she has lost her one last hope.

After half an hour Monica came to her senses and when she opened her eyes, she saw that both of then i.e. Monica and the young girl were tied with ropes. Both the girls were tortured and were made to do things forcefully. Both the girls were raped. In the act of saving the young girl Monica also became the victim of the inhuman act. After struggling a lot, the young girl died at the spot and Monica was broken till the core, she was very ashamed that even after being so strong and having super powers she could not save herself as well as the girl. She left the planet at once and nobody ever saw her again. The mother of the young girl kept waiting for her child, but she never came back home.

Already feeling like I am dead

Already feeling like I'm dead
But I really wanted to live
I collected all my tears in the thread
But the world still have so much pain to give

I was feeling like they buried me alive
Instead in the stream of blood I would have dived

SEVEN

After a week It was the day when Alex had a match, and he was really excited because today he thought he would meet his friend Monica. But the match was about to start but Monica didn't come. He tried to call her many times, but no one responded. He was very much disappointed and worried too because she was not answering the calls. So, after his game was over, he decided to go to the hospital. When he went there, he came the know that Monica have not come to the hospital from 1 week. He was so much worried that something is surely wrong. He searched for her everywhere he could and finally found nothing but a watch falling on the road and remembered that it was of Monica. He searched more and reached the place where all that incident happened and found a letter.

it was written on the top for Alex from Monica.

He read the letter...

Dear Alex,

I don't know it's the right time to tell you all this or not but as you are my only friend on earth so I think I must tell it to you before leaving. I remember once you asked me that why do I always change the topic when you ask me about cape-town but today I want to tell you that that is because I am not like you, I don't belong to this planet earth. I don't know you will believe me or not, but I am an Alien and I belong to planet

cape-town and came I to planet earth only to study about the people of earth.

The news about the spaceship and the alien was all true... the spaceship that appeared few days back in the sky was mine and I came from that spaceship. I wanted to tell it to you before, but I couldn't.

But now because I have gone back to my planet so don't think that we are no more friends. You will be my friend on earth forever.

I also wanted to tell you that something really bad happened with me before I left the planet, I had made many good memories with you and all the people in the hospital. But I don't think that I can ever forget all those bad memories and everything that happened with me and could ever come back.

Will miss you all!

Monica

After reading this letter Alex burst into tears. He felt bad not only because his friend has left the planet but because he could not help her friend in her bad times and from everything that happened with her. He was so much broken because he was not with her friend when she needed him the most. It didn't matter for him weather she was an alien, but she was his good friend.

Months passed...... but he never forgot her, he used to look at stars every night with the hope that one day she would come back and tell, actually was happened with her so that they could the person, but Monica never came back maybe because she was so much dispirited after everything that happened with her and the young girl.

REAL MEN DON'T
RAPE!
I AM
NOT FOR SALE
BLAME THE
SYSTEM NOT THE
VICTIM
City OF Fear

Goodbyes are sad
And sometimes very hard
Goodbyes are regretful
When you really want to start
Sometimes we don't want to say them
But situations make us do the same
Sometimes we really want to stay
But we only end up to claim
But it just ends up becoming a matter of shame

So, this was the story of the two girls. One who never came back because she died and left the world and the other who could not bear the cruelty of this world and left this planet. A sad but bitter truth of our society......

So at last I just want to make an appeal from all of you to make this world a better place for our mothers, sisters, friends, wives and daughters.........because we don't want more girls WHO NEVER COME BACK!

Message from the author

Hello to everyone reading this book, first of all I would like to thank you for buying my book and reading it till the end. Thank you so much for supporting me, and I hope you keep on supporting me in the future as well...

This story, "The Girl who never came back" is not just a story but it hides many morals, many emotions and also many bitter truths in it.

Through this fiction story I just don't want to point only on the current scenarios but the thing which always used to occur in the past as well in different forms.

Today only due to social media everyone knows about the situation and the incidents.

Everyone thinks that if a women is physically, mentally emotionally and economically strong so nothing like this would happen but looking at the current situations we cannot call it true, today women are strong, independent and are not dependent for money on anyone but still all this rape cases that we heard daily still hasn't stop.

So, through this story I want to give you all a message.....

Taking the example of my story: the young girl we can say was a girl from the past (who doesn't have any kind of super-powers) like the girls in the past she was dependent and week. And the alien girl was the girl from the present (she was having super-powers) she was independent and strong but still both of them became the victim of the same thing.

It's not that women have to bring a change in them and become stronger but it is men who have to change and learn to respect a women.. because if the men doesn't change so the strongest women and even the super-powers can't save lives. This story has a sad ending but I hope this will help some struggling women to fight and the message I wanted to give you will help our society to change and will help these women to have a happy ending in their real life stories.

"To every boy or men reading this book, we need your help to change the society."

Thank you!

Thank you note to the publisher

I want to thank Penaaki Publication for helping me publish my first book. I will never forget the happiness of seeing my very first published book!

Thank you for helping me to enter the world of published authors. Penaaki Publications is one of the best platform for all budding writers. I feel so overwhelmed to be the part of it now and I believe it's going to make, inspire and help more people to write, and it will definitely keep bringing amazing content for you in the future as well.

Note from the author

It means a lot to me that the one holding this book right now has bought my book and read it till the end. Words will never be enough to describe how thankful I am. But I'll just say thank you even though I know it is not enough. But I would love to hear from you. You can write to me on writeupsbyangel@gmail.com

Or you can connect with me on Instagram (angels_creation123). I promise I'll reply.

Thank you all for being the part of the beginning of my journey with my first book. Hope you liked my book. Looking forward to write more amazing content for you all.

9 798888 498798

Printed by Libri Plureos GmbH in Hamburg,
Germany